a·Dragon·in·a·Wagon

Lynley Dodd

Gareth Stevens Publishing
Milwaukee

Susie Fogg
took Sam her dog
along by Jackson's Stream.
And as they walked
Susie talked,
and dreamed a wishful
dream.

"Sam," she said,
"You're very good,
you never bark or bite.
The holes you dig
are not TOO big,
and you're always home
at night.
But just for once
it might be fun
if you changed from dog," she said.
"To something HUGE
or something FIERCE
or something ODD
instead.

Let me see,
you could be...
a dragon
in a wagon,

a bat
with a hat,

a snake
eating cake,

a gnu
with the flu,

a whale
in a pail,

a giraffe
with a scarf,

a chimp
with a limp,

a yak
on his back,

a moose
on the loose,

a lizard
in a blizzard

or a shark
in the dark."

A mossy log
tripped Susie Fogg,
she tumbled to the ground.
And as she wiped off
all the mud,
she looked behind
and found...

No sharks, no bats,
no hairy yaks,
no dragons in a jam.
Just the face,
the friendly face,
the DOGGY face
of Sam.

By Lynley Dodd:

GOLD STAR FIRST READERS

Hairy Maclary from Donaldson's Dairy   The Apple Tree
Hairy Maclary's Bone   The Smallest Turtle
Hairy Maclary Scattercat   Wake Up, Bear
Hairy Maclary's Caterwaul Caper   A Dragon in a Wagon

Library of Congress Cataloging-in-Publication Data

Dodd, Lynley.
   A dragon in a wagon.

   (Gold star first readers)
   Summary: For the sake of variety, Susie imagines that her friendly dog
Sam is a series of more exotic creatures, from a dragon in a wagon to a
shark in the dark.
   [1. Dogs — Fiction. 2. Imagination — Fiction. 3. Animals — Fiction. 4.
Stories in rhyme]
   I. Title. II. Series.
PZ8.3.D637Dr   1988   [E]   88-42925
ISBN 1-55532-911-X

North American edition first published in 1988 by

Gareth Stevens, Inc.
7317 West Green Tree Road
Milwaukee, Wisconsin 53223, USA

First published in New Zealand by Mallinson Rendel Publishers Ltd.

1 2 3 4 5 6 7 8 9 94 93 92 91 90 89 88